NEW HAVEN FREE PUBLIC LIBRARY

3 5000 06884 0098

P9-AQQ-827

DATE DUE

MAY 1 9 2001	APR 0 1 2006	FEB 0 9 2013
NOV 1 3 2001	FEB 0 7 2007	
DEC 0 6 2001	NOV 0 9 2007	MAR 1 3 2013
		JAN 2 5 2014
		APR 1 1 2016
JAN 2 0 2008	JAN 1 4 2008	
JAN 1 0 2004	JAN 0 5 2009	
	FEB 0 3 2009	
JUN 1 2004		
JAN 1 8 2005		
FEB 0 3 2005	MAR 2 8 2009	
MAR 0 1 2005	MAR 1 2 2011	
JAN 1 1 2006		
	JAN 2 4 2013	

LUCILLE'S SNOWSUIT

by Kathryn Lasky   illustrated by Marylin Hafner

Crown Publishers ♕ New York

For my friends Molly and Meghan
—K.L.

For Abigail, Jennifer, and Amanda—
who remember those sweaty snowsuits!
—M.H.

Text copyright © 2000 by Kathryn Lasky
Illustrations copyright © 2000 by Marylin Hafner

All rights reserved. No part of this book may be reproduced or transmitted in any form or by any means, electronic
or mechanical, including photocopying, recording, or by any information storage and retrieval system,
without permission in writing from the publisher.

Published by Crown Publishers, a division of Random House, Inc.,
1540 Broadway, New York, New York 10036.

CROWN and colophon are trademarks of Random House, Inc.

www.randomhouse.com/kids

Library of Congress Cataloging-in-Publication Data
Kathryn Lasky.
Lucille's snowsuit / by Kathryn Lasky ; illustrations by Marylin Hafner.
p.   cm.
Summary: Lucille has so much trouble getting her snowsuit on that she is almost too
tired to go outside and join her brother and sister playing in the snow.

ISBN 0-517-80037-3 (trade) — 0-517-80038-1 (lib. bdg.)

[1. Clothing and dress—Fiction. 2. Snow—Fiction. 3. Brothers and sisters—Fiction. 4. Pigs—Fiction.]
I. Hafner, Marylin, ill. II. Title.

PZ7.L3274 Lr 2000
[E]—dc21

99-462101

Printed in Singapore

10   9   8   7   6   5   4   3   2   1

September 2000

First Edition

"Guess what, Lucille?" said
Lucille's older brother, Franklin.
"What?" said Lucille.
"It's a snow day! No school."

"I don't go to school," said Lucille.

"Don't you want to play in the snow?" said her older sister, Frances. "Get your snowsuit on. We're going out."

Franklin and Frances rushed out the door
and pounced into a huge pile of snow.

Lucille was left behind. First she pulled on
her boots. Then she got out her snowsuit.
She climbed in. She stood up. She pulled.
Nothing happened. **Boots first! Big mistake,**
Lucille thought. She pulled harder.

*"**Mommy!**"* called Lucille.

"I'll be right there, dear," her mother called from upstairs. Lucille pulled and pulled. She couldn't get her boots through the legs, and she couldn't pull them out to start over again. She was *really* stuck.

"MOMMY!" she yelled.

"Just one more minute."

Lucille pulled down the snowsuit legs and yanked. Her foot came out, but not her boot. She yanked and yanked. Finally her boot came out. Lucille was sweating and she was tired.

She took a little rest before trying again. Then she stood up and stepped into the snowsuit. She pulled it all the way up and put her arms in the sleeves. Then she pulled the zipper. It stuck.

Lucille lay down half zipped. A snowball
sailed by the window. She could hear
Frances and Franklin laughing, shouting.
I bet they aren't sweating, she thought.

"I hate snowsuits! Snowsuits are for babies.
I am *not* a baby!" She pulled on the hood. It
was itchy. She felt something lumpy in her
pant leg.

"MOMMY!"

"Here I am. *Now* what's wrong, Lucille?"

"I'm hot. I'm sweating. My sock's lost. My

zipper's stuck. *I hate snowsuits!*" Lucille roared.

"You have to wear your snowsuit, dear."

"I want to wear a parka like Frances and Franklin and ski pants with a stripe on each leg and a hat with a bouncy ball on top."

"A snowsuit is best. When you get bigger, you can wear Frances's parka and ski pants."

"Snowsuits are for babies."

"Snowsuits keep you warmer when you're little. You have to wear yours."

"No, I don't. I'll go naked," said Lucille.

"You'll freeze," said her mother.

"I won't. I'm sweating."

Lucille's mother found the sock, unstuck Lucille's zipper, snapped the snaps of her hood, untangled her mitten strings, and put on her boots. "Now you're ready to go outside!"

Lucille flopped down flat. "I can't," she said.

"Why not?"

"Too tired." Lucille's hood felt so tight.
She thought about hats with fluffy balls
that jiggled.

"Get up, Lucille."

Lucille thought about ski pants with stripes.

"I need a lemonade."

"Lucille. It's winter."

"I'm sweating," Lucille said.

"Go make a snowman," her mother said.

"I want to go swimming."

Frances and Franklin came inside to see where Lucille was.

"Lucille, what are you doing on the floor?" Frances asked.

"Come out and help with the snowman," Franklin said.

"I can't."

"Why not?" Frances asked.

"My snowsuit is too hot. I need ski pants and a parka and a hat with a fluffy ball. Snowsuits are for babies."

"No snowsuit, no snow play," said Frances.

"Simple as that. Now get up, Lucille."

"Carry me."

"All right," Franklin said.

They carried Lucille outside and plopped her in the snow.
Lucille swung her arms. Snow angels!

She closed her eyes and let the snow float down on her
eyelashes. Then she opened them and watched the sky
through snowflaky eyes. Soon she began to cool down.

Franklin dropped a snowball on her chest.
"Snowball fight!" he yelled, and ran away.

Lucille jumped up. She made a snowball
and threw it at her brother. Frances made
one and threw it at Lucille; then Franklin
made one and threw it at Frances. Soon
snowballs were whizzing through the air.
Frances and Franklin lost their hats. Lucille
found them and filled them with snow.
They put them on and yowled.

Lucille laughed.

"I'm going in. I'm freezing," Franklin said.

"Me too," said Frances.

"Not me," said Lucille.

Lucille stood up, flopped on the sled, and
went down the hill lickety-split. She squealed
and did it again. Her hood unsnapped and the
air whistled by her ears.

When Franklin and Frances had warmed up and
come out again, they all went triple on the sled.

"We're the toast, you're the butter!" Frances and
Franklin shouted as they whizzed down the hill.
For Lucille was in the middle between them. Not
too cold and not too warm.

"Mommy, guess what? My snowsuit kept
me snuggly warm and I didn't even sweat."

FEB   2001